ZeaZoo & the Land of Boo

" An Urban Fairytale "

By P.D. Blackmon

P. D. Blackmon

iAmerica Soul
Indigenous American Publishing

This book is dedicated in loving memory of my Dad, Mom And Grandmother, my Moral Compass and Undeniable Hero's!

My inspiration in life and for this book remains my two most precious accomplishment of all time, My son Lamar and grandson.

It is also dedicated to the children and parents of the world. God bless us All.

A special Thank You to Danielle Holland, and Lee Baley.

Table of Content

INTRODUCTION

ZeaZoo & the Land of Boo is an *"Urban Fairytale"* the first in a series of "family-friendly" eBooks.

Zea a disenchanted, boy from Bay Village (Gulf Coast), nearly drowns in the Karina Hurricane. Awakening in the Land of Boo, a magical wonderland under the sea, he befriends unique magical characters that help him try and get back home to save his family and friends; all while trying to stay one step ahead of the vengeful Nino, King of Soul, Queen Elvia, and the royal Boo security, along with the SeaWeeds, who seek revenge and his death.

IT'S ABOUT LOVE, FAITH, AND FAMILY

The Land of Boo is about love, family, honor, and faith prevailing against all odds, conquering all fears, and realizing *all that glitters is not gold*. Soon, Zea will understand that knowledge and wisdom are the most precious gifts of all. With it, he will be protected, loved, and watched over forever.

Though it may cost all he has, he must understand, he must seek and obtain knowledge. The theme can be expressed as: love, family, honor, and faith, conquers all.

"Money Can't Buy You Love."

CHARACTERS:

Isaiah "ZeaZoo" Blue

A handsome boy 13 years of age, a *dreamer* always looking for the ultimate "pie in the sky," something better than his boring life in Bay Village, he is highly intelligent, a straight-A student, something he keeps on the "down-low". (Very un-cool to be smart). Although he is a great student, he has his heart set on becoming a "gangsta" and joining the infamous X Gang, fast girls, and fast cars, fast cash. His mother wants him to be a doctor or maybe even President.

Mika "Mae Mae"

Dubois the prettiest girl in Bay Village, fourteen years of age, witty, smart, and slightly stuck on herself, most popular girl in school and head cheerleader for the Bay Village Panthers Football team. Sometimes making poor decisions, not confident putting her hopes, dreams, and future in the hands of someone else, she is secretly in love with Ben Boo.

Magic Monroe

is a free-spirited kind boy with great possibilities. One of Zea's best friends. He's the true clown in the group.

Rasta Man

is a community organizer, delightfully funny guy with wisdom and knowledge.

Bennie Boo

Leader of the X Gang, the largest gang on the Gulf Coast.

Choir Boy

Is highly spiritual. He can quote the Bible in a heartbeat. He's a deep thinker and the philosopher of the group a "PK" Preacher's Kid.

Essay Lopez

Zea's best friend, a delightful boy, with a heart of gold.

Lady Di

Ruler of Boo East.

Enchantress O aka Lady O

Grand Ruler lives in the capital city of Boo. She has magical powers and the granter of all wishes.

Magnolia

A beautiful human /hybrid fairy butterfly angel, with magical powers, has a "take no prisoners" attitude. She changes colors with her mood swings.

Queen Crysta

Deceased wife of King Nino.

Elvia Queen of Soul Human/Mermaid hybrid

Sister to Queen Crystal, once was the sister-in-law to King Nino, with magical powers. She can swim the ocean and walk the land. She seeks revenge for the death of her sister Queen Crystal and the "Black Medallion" believed stolen.

Nino King of Soul Human/Merman hybrid

Ruler of the deep-blue sea, heart-broken beloved husband of the now-deceased Queen Crystal. Revenge is the only thing on his mind.

The Lost Girls

are the Human Mermaids with special powers.

Bubbles the Whale

is the Official Press Secretary for the Land of Boo.

King Fish

Smooth operator - a shark.

Soul Bro #1 and Soul Bro #2

are King Fish's shark army of thugs.

The Silvers SeaWeeds

are the royal informants.

Willie Popcorn and EyesWorth Green

are the Royal Boo Land Security and Armed Forces.

CHAPTER I

THE MYSTERIOUS PACKAGE

It's a beautiful day although a storm is predicted, there's no sign, just another summer day in Bay Village Park the Saturday before Katrina is scheduled to hit the Gulf Coast. Bennie Boo and the X Gang pull up and walk towards Zea and his best friends Choir Boy, Magic Monroe, and Essay casually kicking it, close by his sister and brother play and sing "Once upon a time in the Land of Boo there lived a little boy name "ZeaZoo" the kids sing in harmony. "Grow up" snaps Zea, now in deep thought, he is being seduced into a possible life of crime and has been pressured into passing a gang initiation, a task created by gang leader Bennie Boo to show his loyalty. Bennie's Lieutenant points at Zea approaches him and hands him a *secret package*. He is to deliver it to 231 Contra Street. For his trouble, he will be given cash and the privilege of joining the gang. This is Zea's chance to prove himself to Bennie and a chance to pick up some fast easy cash.

But there is a problem, something goes wrong a rival gang approaches him when he mistakenly travels onto their turf and the chase is on. After running through the alley, across the park, jumping a fence, Zea somehow loses the gang members chasing him and the mysterious package. He knows he is in danger, perspiration dripping down his face.

His head is pounding with the thought that now he must face the wrath of Bennie because this is The Land of Boo.

Now that he is being hunted by Boo and on the run, he needs to make it to Rasta Man who will know what to do. As he approaches Rasta's shop, he spots Bennie and the Gang headed in his direction and starts to run, he hears gunshots flying past his head as he bobs and weaves. Rasta sees what's happening and intervenes. "This is my world," shouts Bennie as he speeds away, knowing it's not wise to mess with the Rasta Man. Everyone knows he's a little crazy. Zea tells Rasta Man what has happened and why Bennie is chasing and trying to kill him, but Rasta wants no part of the gangs or violence and declines, not wanting to get involved. But Bennie has given Zea 24 hours to find his package or else, he is doomed. What will he do?

Mika "Mae Mae" Dubois (prettiest girl in Bay Village) and head cheerleader for the Bay Village Panthers Football team and her girls are practicing their high-flying routine when she tells them her secret. She loves Bennie Boo, she thinks. *Although there is a storm on the horizon the girls,* have no worries.

THE GRASS IS ALWAYS GREENER ON THE OTHERSIDE

The evening before Katrina hits the Gulf Coast, and Mom and Dad Blue, Zea's parents, sisters, brother, his grandparents Nana and Paw Paw, Reverend, and First Lady, Choir Boy, Magic, are all having their traditional Sunday dinner at Magnolias Sea Food Restaurant owned by the families. The subject of discussion is the family business, a successful restaurant located on Bourbon Street in the French Quarters. What is the plan of action? The question on everybody's mind. TV News can be heard in the background, the Mayor of Bay Village is speaking and looking extremely worried. The Police Chief is again calling for mandatory evacuation. Sitting at the table texting is ZeaZoo, a nickname Isaiah's Nana had given him at birth, he is checking his messages and the hurricane alert app. Shaking his head in concern, he is not so sure if it's best for his family to stay.

In his head, he knows he should insist that they pack up and leave but, in his heart, he knows he can't go. Although Zea lives in Bay Village Estates a beautiful beachfront community on the Gulf Coast, he still dreams of a gangster's paradise, fast cars, fast girls, and fast cash. Zea and his boys are playing their new game while contemplating their future hopes, dreams, aspirations, and many options. Zea interrupts to tell them he has decided to join the infamous Z Gang, but only temporarily, just to make some fast cash so he can win the heart of Mika "Mae Mae" Dubois, the prettiest girl in Bay Village, whom he has loved since the third grade. Although Mika likes Zea as a friend, she has always had her eyes on "big baller" Bennie Boo, top gangsta and Bay Village's most infamous native.

A mandatory evacuation of all Bay Village residents is the call again from city officials, but as with the Blues, some residents on the Gulf Coast are not preparing to evacuate. They have lived through the last great hurricane and believe like many here they will be able to ride this one out as well. By Sunday night the call for mandatory evacuation from city officials have turned to horror. An apocalyptic fate was being predicted for anyone who dared to stay. Everyone needs to get out now! The Blues and Monroe families have finally decided it is time to leave. Zea calls Mae Mae they will pick her and her mother up on their way out of town.

BLOOD IS THICKER THAN WATER

It's settled, they are leaving, after gathering a few of their most precious memories, they all head out of town. Because of their last-minute decision to depart the city, they are now trapped on the freeway with thousands of others, attempting to flee in-pending doom.

While riding in the car, Zea is thinking of what happened earlier. Flashing back, he is on pins and needles on the lookout and down low frightened by the fact that Bennie and the X Gang are now hunting him. He must find the mysterious package he has lost and return it ASAP, or he is in monumental trouble. Thinking about the advice of his friends, Zea has decided that the "gangsta life" is not for him. What had he been thinking? He had been brought up in a great family and he was going to tell them all, he had been temporarily blinded by fake and false illusions of grandeur "bling-bling".

Zea's friend and mentor Rasta Man is the only one that can help him now, everyone knows he's a little crazy and not to be played with. He is respected for his knowledge, wisdom, and heart, his no-nonsense approach to life and death. Rasta has convinced Zea not to get involved with the X Gang, giving him money to cover his debt of the mysterious package. However, they all are running out of time as the Karina Hurricane grows near.

All residents who have not been able to evacuate are preparing as best they can for the pending hurricane headed for the Gulf Coast. Tick tock...

Hurricane Katrina struck the Gulf Coast, a category 5, with sustained winds of 140 miles per hour, stretching over 400 miles. Vicious and brutal, widespread flooding, complete devastation. The sounds of glass shattering, gas lines bursting into flames, was witnessed as the disaster scene unfolds in Bay Village. Everybody is in a panic and have the same fears, "We're all going to die..."

EVERYMAN FOR HIMSELF GOD FOR US ALL

There is panic in the air everyone is in a state of shock, wandering around the streets and vacant lots where their homes once stood, dazed. It looks like a war zone and the residents resemble war victims. The winds are howling with severe rain, but there seems to be a lull in the storm. "It's time to go.", shouts Mrs. Blue. Her brother in Houston begged her to come up before Katrina hit.

During the commotion, Zea is being dragged to the car by his father. He knows that they only have a short window of opportunity to get out. They are in the eye of the storm and the momentary calm would soon be replaced by the back wall of the hurricane which could bring with its severe storm surges. He hastily shoves him into the car. Zea is trying to explain what's going on with Mika but with all the confusion and hysteria gets drowned out. Just as the family starts down the driveway, Zea bolts from the car and runs to the partially destroyed garage door. Seeing his new birthday present for the first time, a motorbike, this is his ticket out. Hopping on it, he heads towards Mae Mae's house. Ms. Blue and the family are hysterical. They start to follow Zea in the car. A huge tree and telephone pole crash down and block both cars. There is no way out. They are trapped. At that moment, a 100-foot wall of water, a tsunami, tosses their cars like Hot Wheels.

IT'S GOING TO TAKE A MIRACLE

Meanwhile, Zea has reached Mae Mae's house and she and her mother are safe for now, but not for long. A wall of water smashes into the home and sweeps them all away. Thrown and tossed into the murky waters, huge waves battering their nearly drowned bodies until they almost lose consciousness. A massive endless sea of debris, trees, cars, furniture, TV sets, and Mika's mother pass. Zea trying to hold onto Mika grabs her and her mother. One moment they are all in his arms, the next moment they were gone. The only way to survive now is to hold his breath until the waves wash over him. He takes a deep breath and prays for his survival. On Shoreline Drive, the families' cars are struck by the 100-foot waves as they are being washed away.

At Abundant Blessings Church, Rev., Choir Boy, and First Lady are also trapped at the church sanctuary which is being washed away. At that moment, a surge of water breaks down the church door. They try to outrun the fast-moving waves and are swept up and off their feet. Rasta Man is also trying to survive. His roof has been blown off. His store is in shambles and he needs to get to a safe place. He packs up his pets and starts to leave when a wall of water smashes through his front glass window and sweeps him away too.

Bennie Boo and the X Gang, headed by car across the Bay Village Bridge are met by a wall of water, as they search for Zea vanishing from sight. They join thousands of others now fighting for their lives.

MONEY CAN'T BUY YOU LOVE

Hurricane Katrina is causing mass destruction in the "open sea" as well as on the Gulf Coast. The waters are unseasonable warm, a strong indicator to all sea creatures that impending danger is imminent. The mermaids and mermen are experiencing the devastation of catastrophic proportion. Katrina is creating underwater volcanoes, earthquakes, and tsunamis as predicted in the ancient sea scrolls. Written 251 million years ago, it tells of the "greatest disaster of all times." 96% of all sharks and marine species were wiped out, known as the "Permian Mass Extinction" a time of "Great Dying" and it is happening again. The prophecy is coming true; as written one day an alien invasion would take place conducted by a primitive civilization, believers of war, petty prejudices, greed, and mass destruction (global warming), marking the beginning of total initialization of the open ocean. A mortal enemy who has hunted our ancestors, cousins, whales, sharks, and dolphins among others to the brink (in some cases) of extinction, barbaric savages who eat them for food and hunt them for sport. During the natural disaster Queen Crystal (Sea of Blood) is killed (she co-rules along with her husband Nino, the King of Soul (Black Sea), and sister, Elvia Queen of Soul. They are livid over the death of Queen Crystal not realizing it was a natural disaster that caused his beloved wife's untimely death.

Empowered by all the forces of the "Sea Gods" they will avenge the late Queen's death. It was all coming to pass as told for generations. An alien would one day walk from the sea and with him death and destruction shall follow...

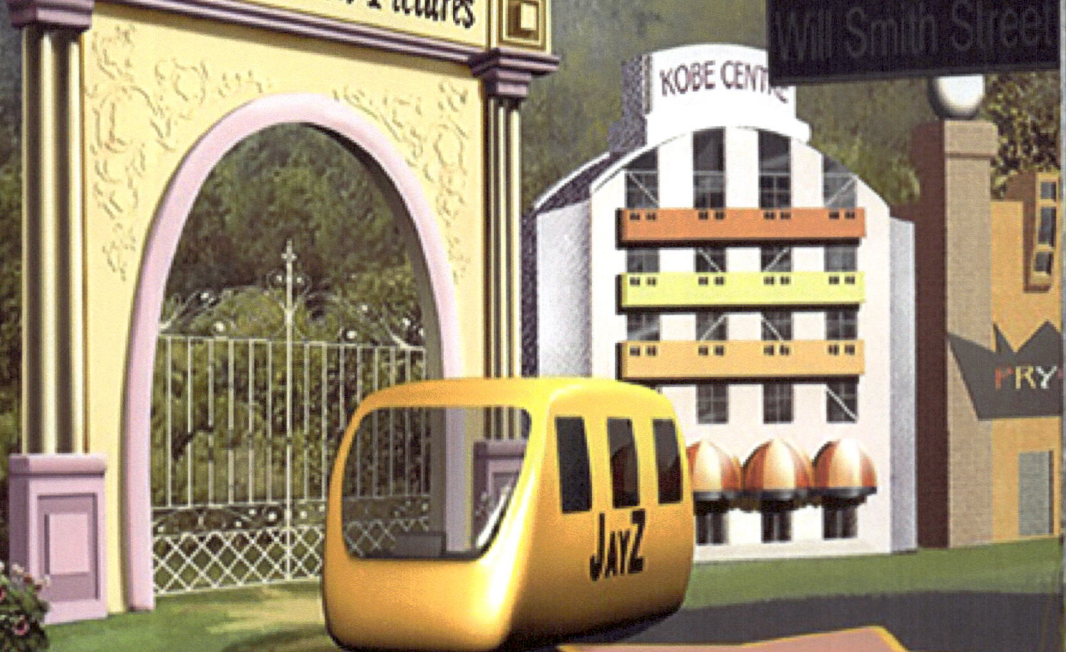

CHAPTER II

During Zea's ordeal, swept away by huge waves and fighting for his life, he has lost sight of Mae Mae and her mother. He is surely about to die. Going down for the third time, a mysterious magical hand wearing a unique watch reaches out of nowhere. Zea thinks to himself, "Could this be the hand of God?" Flashing back on good times, that thought is quickly interrupted by Bennie Boo chasing him with a gun.

He awakens on an unknown shore in an unknown land. Is he dead? Is this Heaven? Or worst yet (he should have prayed more) is this Hell? As he stands, he realizes he no longer needs his glasses something he has needed since third grade. And what he sees is breathtakingly beautiful, and magical.

FAMILY FRIENDLY FILMS PRESENTS

ZERZOO &
LAND OF BOO

"an adventure from y tale"

WELCOME TO THE LAND OF BOO

To his amazement, the sea splits, and riding on a borrow wave is a beautiful princess. She is Lady Di, ruler of Society Hills in the Land of Boo. She smiles and raises her arms in a welcoming gesture and asks, "Do you come in peace"? "Welcome to the Land of Boo" Zea, confused and in shock and still a little woozy from his near-drowning experience, is filled with a thousand questions. He explains that he is from Bay Village, not knowing exactly where he is or how he got there. He and his family had been in a great storm and he needed to get back to help and find out their fate. This must be the end of the world or

worst, Hell he thinks. With an assuring smile, Princess Di beckons all the Land of Boo children to come out of hiding. With that, everyone cheers and begins dancing and singing in the streets. "Hip Hop Hooray, ho, hey", they all sang with joy. Princess Di explains he has miraculously killed Queen Crystal the wife of Nino, King of Soul, that she was beloved by the king and all their followers. "Zea you are in trouble boy.", warns Lady Di.

His only hope of ever getting back home lies in the mythical city of gold and crystals, the Lost City of Atlantis. He must go and see Enchantress O, granter of all miracles in the Land of Boo. However, his journey will be filled with danger. She explains that he is being hunted by the King and Queen along with Boo Secret Service the SeaWeeds, their loyal royal informants. They seek revenge for the death of Queen Crystal and the Magical Medallion that she wore around her neck. Zea is perplexed. He has never killed anyone, and he knows nothing of a magic medallion.

Lady Di explains the Urban Legend of the Sea. "It was written that one day the oceans would warm turning boiling hot and there would be catastrophic devastation and the arrival of an alien would follow. There is the devastation and here you are. So, the urban tale indeed must be true. But first you must travel to Never Ever Land. Be careful!", she warns. "It's guarded by the revolutionary Black Panthers. Just follow the Bimini Road and believe." She whispers as she returns to the sea in the same manner and way in which she came.

DESTINATION NEVER EVER LAND: WHAT TIME IS IT?

As Zea follows the Bimini Road, illuminated by stars on the street in the direction of the kingdom of Atlantis, he comes upon a church and to his surprise Choir Boy is conducting the choir. The boys do not recognize each other from before. They are meeting for the first time. Choir Boy not knowing how he got to the Land of Boo either - the two set off towards Never Ever Land.

Just then four sets of eyes appear out of the darkness one set of blue eyes set, of green one set of gold. Like ghosts in an instant three sets of snarling, growling sharp-pointed teeth also come into view. This is their worst nightmare. They are about to be killed and eaten by three ferocious animals. The panthers capture the boys after chasing them both down. Zea and Choir Boy pass out and awaken in a strange place. A dark shadow appears (face of Rasta Man) and walks towards them. As he approaches, he speaks. "What's up Huey?" the Panthers now in full view are snarling at the kids. Responding to his words, the big black cats' faces instantly turn to glee. Their collars in full view now with the names Huey, Afeni and Tupac printed in precious stones. "Who have you brought me?", asks the Mysterious Stranger.

The dangerous cats' demeanor instantly turns completely pleasant. Huey explains they found the boys wandering around the entrance to the Golden Gate thinking they might be enemies, of the state. The other Panthers begin to talk of their confusion and possible potential danger the strangers could bring to Angel Falls. After passing the first test Rasta Man and Huey share the secrets of Boo and give him a magical watch for protection. He has 48 hours to make it to the City of Gold and Crystals.

Once there, Enchantress O would grant all their wishes. After 48 hours the magical watch will lose all magical powers. Foreseeing danger, Rasta Man also commissions Magnolia, a magically beautiful human butterfly to secretly follow the boys for extra protection. Looking through a huge plasma flat screen they see that the King and Queen of Soul were hot on the trail. They must hurry. They must go now!

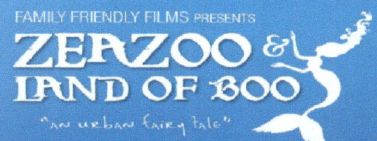

FAMILY FRIENDLY FILMS PRESENTS

ZERZOO &
LAND OF BOO

"an urban fairy tale"

LOST

While in Never Ever Land, the boys run into a beautiful young girl with a small child. She is crying and highly distressed, apparently lost and abandoned. As Zea approaches, the stranger looks up between her tears she says, her name is Gia. She has been waiting for weeks for her boyfriend to return and pick her up to no avail. She has put all of her hopes and dreams in the hands of someone other than herself and is now wondering if that was the right thing to do. She begins to question her past. Struggling with her low self-esteem and an inner quest to be loved. She does not recognize her intellect, inner or outer beauty. When Gia looks at her reflection in the lake of water, she does not see what everyone else sees (a beautiful intelligent girl). When she looks, all she sees is an ugly, fat, unworthy image. Zea and Choir Boy invite her to accompany them to Atlantis East maybe O can help her too. Now Gia an around the way girl is no stranger to danger. Though she did not realize it yet quite capable of fulfilling her own dreams. So, without hesitation, she stands and agrees, "Let's Roll!", she shouts as she walks with confidence. They all jump into Zea's magical car and proceed.

FORK IN THE ROAD OF LIFE

A few miles down Bimini Road, the stars miraculously re-appear coming to a fork in the road with three different directions, the group pauses. Which road shall they travel now? In the distance they see the Boo Travel Agency. As they enter the establishment Zea greets the stranger and asks for help. As they enter the establishment, Zea greets the stranger who have the (Face of Essay) and asks for help. The stranger tells them his name is Angel, the owner of the Boo Travel Agency. Zea explains they were on their way to the City of Gold and need directions. The confused stranger points in one direction, then the other, than all directions at once. Angel confesses to the group he is having issues and is struggling with his mental capacity. He is feeling close to a breakdown. After hearing the kids were on their way to see Enchantress O it is settled without invitation Angel is going too.

Just up the hill on top of a huge cliff, next to a posted "bungee jump" sign, someone has a bungee jump cord wrapped around their ankle and is beating himself up. Upon further observation, it appears he is having a fistfight with himself. As Zea walks forward, Magic Monroe's face comes into view however the boys do not recognize each other. "What's up? Are you OK?", yells Zea. "My name is MJ, I'm so disappointed in myself.", he pouted as he slaps himself in the face. Only stopping momentarily, explaining that he and his girlfriend and a bunch of other kids, all were here earlier to see him make the highest bungee jump in Boo history. He was so scared he was unable to complete the task. He did not have the nerve and could not do it. He had no heart, no courage. Feeling his pain, Zea invites him to journey with them to the Capitol City maybe O can help him find courage.

TRAPPED AND ABOUT TO DIE

Darkness falls over the Land of Boo. The evil King and Queen of Soul have trapped the kids in an old, abandoned house. Their faces appear like magic and they walk through the dimensions separating water and land. Approaching the group, Elvia tells them that Zea has killed her sister and stolen has the Black Medallion from them. They want it back now or prepare to die. Gia, MJ, Angel, and Choir Boy are terrified. Zea tries to fend off the evil crew, but he was no match. Just when it looks like the end is near, Magnolia appears to their surprise. She has been following them, orders of the Mysterious Stranger for extra protection. Changing colors and shooting lightning bolts, she distracts the evil group, shocking them over and over again with a mighty force of electricity as she circles the room. Zea seeing the anger in the royal pair's eyes anticipates grave trouble and tries to distract them but they had Magnolia in their vengeful sights. Her power is no match for King Nino or Queen Elvia. They shoot back both with the same motion, a huge lightning bolt that's five times bigger striking Magnolia, in the heart. She falls from the sky but before hitting the ground - she vanishes.

The kids now in shock over the death of their beloved Magnolia hover in the center of the room. The King flanked by Queen Elvia and the others approach, reaching for the medallion hanging around Zea's neck. Queen Elvia receiving a forceful shock is thrown off her feet, burning her nails, hair, eyelashes, and hands. Gathering her composure Elvia raises her hand to retaliate. At that moment, a star appears. On the star, sits Princess Di laughing out loud and shaking her finger. "Not on my watch!", says Lady Di. In a soft, fading voice "Not on my watch..." Angry, shocked, and surprised, Elvia is still burning. King Nino is blowing his breath on her trying to completely put the fire out consuming her clothes. Rubbing her backside, the Queen threatens the kids and tells Zea to watch his back. "You too will pay." With that prophecy, they all make-a-dash and jump back through the force field dividing the two lands leading to the 7th dimension, their secret entrance to the sea. Upon penetrating the invisible wall and transforming back to mermaids and mermen they all swim away.

Sad and confused, Zea is sorry he could not save Magnolia. If he were bigger or stronger, he could have done more to save her from death at the hands of the evil King and Queen. Starting to question himself, wondering if they would ever make it to Atlantis East with such an evil posse trying to capture and kill them. The odds didn't look good and he knew it.

BAD BOY, WHAT YOU GONNA DO WHEN THEY COME FOR YOU?

Entering the valley below the cliffs, they see coming out of the sea across the beach three sea and land Rovers loaded with gangs of people. As they approach you can hear the sound of Hip Hop music coming from the sedans. Gia recognizes her boyfriend, X the leader of the Land of Boo's most notorious "OG" Gang, a little info she has selected not to reveal until now. As the entourage surrounds the kids, they demand the return of Gia. Having gained confidence Gia is certain she deserves better and refuses to go. They are apprehended but not before she scratches her attacker.

THE DEATH OF THE BLUES

Zea rushes X and hits the gang leader, turning to pick up Baby Girl, he then continues the fight getting the best of X by tricking him. He uses his brains instead of his muscles. This angers X. Still terribly upset but with a smile he removes an electrical device from his pocket. A visual scene appears in a hologram showing images of Zea's family along with his friends. All are fighting for their lives. They suffer, screaming, drowning, crying, and dying before their very eyes, during the Karina Hurricane. It was far worse than Zea ever imagined breaking out in a cold sweat, in shock and awe, overtakes the moment.

Gia covers her eyes. She begins to shake uncontrollably. Tears are rolling down her eyes. She opens her mouth to cry but there is no sound. No one can speak a word. X, feeling great satisfaction for causing such distress and grief, begins to laugh while his gold tooth sparkles, in the sun. Zea, who is visibly shaken, tries to regain his composure. He charges towards X hitting him in the mouth and knocking off his shaded glasses. X fires back with a left jab and the fight is on. Zea is getting the best of the situation. The other gang members jump in the attack, dragging Zea off the beaten leader while apprehending the rest of the group. After getting up, dusting himself off with a smile, X proclaims to Zea, "This is my world. The Land of Boo!", as he smirks and walks away.

REBIRTH OF MAGNOLIA

Just when all seemed lost, different colors began to appear in the sky, pink, purple, ocean blue, and red. It was Magnolia the beautiful fairy butterfly thought to have been dead until now. Quickly releasing Zea, they both do a coordinated karate move and begin their offensive. Using his magical watch, Zea begins to launch firebombs at X. Magnolia follows and circles the gang wrapping some of them in an invisible rope. She shoots tiny fireballs, whirling them in the direction of the other gang members. While engulfed in flames, the gang members jump into the sea while the others jump back into their Hummers and race across the beach disappearing, in the distance. Zea, exhausted and devastated by the ordeal, mourns, and contemplates the news that his family is dead - all of them. Collapsing on the beach, trying not to show weakness, he stares off into the distance as tears fill his eyes. His family is dead. What will he do? Where will he go? Zea looks at his friends with complete confusion, sadness, anger, and a feeling of being lost. His emotions are engulfing his psyche all at once. He feels it welling up into his throat. He can't swallow. He can't breathe. He can't think. Angel also stunned appears in shock. He's beating his chest with tears streaming down his face. Choir Boy is pacing in silent pain as he relies on his strong faith. He prays out aloud. Gia is repressed. She stares into space, rocking, as she comforts Baby Girl who is upset and is crying uncontrollably. MJ is trying to burn his grief and pain through exercise. He is shadow boxing breaking into his Muhammad Ali impersonation. "We've got to float like a butterfly..." Magnolia demonstrates and stings MJ like a bee.

TO MAKE LIFE IMPORTANT!

Interrupting the moment, Zea questions in a solemn voice, "Why do people die?" The kids turn their focus on Zea giving him their full attention. All are still noticeably quiet and after a long silence, Choir Boy replies, "To make life important!" They all individually nod in sad confirmation. Zea finds inner strength with those words and jumps to his feet followed by Choir Boy, Gia, and the rest of the group.

Appearing over the horizon is the City of Gold and Crystals Atlantis East. There is no turning back now is the troops rallying cry. As Atlantis East comes within full view the singing and dancing begin. The excited group approach the *streets paved with gold* leading to the main entrance, of the Boo Palace. All their wishes will soon be granted. Zea will get to go back to Bay Village. Gia will find love and acceptance. Angel anticipates higher intellect - a brain. MJ will soon receive his heart and courage and Choir Boy his abundant faith. As they approach the grand gate, three large leopards that appear to be statues come to life and start to chase the kids. One of them chases Baby Girl around a tree. The other chases Zea, MJ, and Angel to the edge of a cliff. Gia, who has fallen, jumps to her feet and without thinking slaps the big cat across the nose. Meanwhile, Leopard #2 has cornered the boys at the cliff's edge. MJ sees a vine. He wraps his friends into it and before they knew it flings all of them, over the ledge. Leopard #1 still in shock over being slapped begins to cry. Baby Girl feeling regretful begins to comfort the emotionally wounded big cat. During the commotion, a familiar voice rings out. It's Huey stepping out of the shadows followed by Afeni and Tupac appearing with big smiles from the bush. Composing herself, Leopard #1 explains the situation through her tears. Huey tells her that the kids are here to see Enchantress O and they need her help. By this time Leopard #2 and #3 have returned to listen. The boys have found their way back up the mountain. "Why didn't you say so?", replies the Leopard. "Any friend of Princess Diana and the Mysterious Stranger are friends of ours! Come on in – welcome!"

HAPPY DAYS ARE HERE AGAIN

The huge golden gates fling open. Inside is a fantasyland of great opulence huge skyscrapers, theme parks, and thousands of cheering children. All residents of Atlantis East are singing and dancing. In the middle of the square sits the gigantic "O" Mall. The kids are placed in a tricked-out convertible Rolls Royce where they are driven around the square, in parade fashion. They are taken into the wonderful huge structure. Gia and Baby Girl are greeted by two attendants and taken to the salon. Zea, Choir Boy, MJ, and Angel are taken through another door. A butler prepares their baths and lays out a room full of clothes and gear. As Zea daydreams about never leaving such a fantastic place, his thoughts are abruptly interrupted. What was he thinking? He has got to get back home and help. Magically a golden door appears and opens. It's General Galena Grand Guard for Enchantress O. She is followed by two other royal attendants. Unrolling a scroll, she tells them that they are invited to be Enchantress O's special guests, at the "Sweet Sixteen Ball". With that information, she nods and exits back through the golden door that mysteriously disappears. The next day is the "Sweet Sixteen Royal Ball". Zea and the Crew are all dancing and having a great time anticipating the moment they would finally meet Enchantress O.

DANGER WATCH YOURSELF

In walks X and his gang entourage. Spotting Gia, he grabs her and drags her kicking and screaming towards the exit. Zea charges after X, followed by Choir Boy, MJ, and Angel. During the disruption, no one realizes that the dome holding the underwater sea back surrounding the ballroom has turned dark and ominous. To their amazement King Nino

and Queen Elvia along with their royal security and followers have somehow entered the underwater sanctuary threatening the integrity of the dome. Two of the Lost Girls zap the gang members freezing them in motion. The gang members are turned into glass and have disintegrated right before everyone's eyes. "Surrender Zea!", demands Elvia as a severe crack forms in the dome. "Surrender Zea now!", echoes King Nino followed by another crack. Frighten the "Sweet Sixteen" guests began to scatter in chaos, pandemonium, and fear grips the room. X who has been traumatized has hidden under a table but not before using Baby Girl, as his human shield. Gia, who witnessed the cowardly behavior reaches for her, in the nick of time. Gia swiftly takes her to safety. With all of their chances for an audience with Enchantress O ruined now, Zea and the crew sit in the destroyed ballroom dazed and confused. After all, they were safe for the moment. However, they still need to see the great "O". They did not know if that would ever happen. Gia starts to cry. The boys feel like doing the same. Magnolia and Angel chime in and they all and cry. Choir Boy starts to pray. MJ interrupts with a weak joke. Zea, exhausted by it all, places his head in his hands and says a silent prayer.

NEVER SAY NEVER

Just when all seemed lost, a wall-to-wall plasma screen appears and a room full of General Galena images appears. "Enchantress O will see all of you tomorrow. All of your wishes will be granted." The images disappear. Jumping to their feet, the kids rejoice and celebrate the impending great compassion "Enchantress O" will bestow to them.

The next morning could not come fast enough. The palace attendants assisted the kids with grooming for their audience with "Enchantress O". A large golden door opens, and Galena leads the kids down a long-illuminated hall. Zea leads the group. He grabs hold of Gia's hand, who is holding the hand of Baby Girl, who holds Choir Boy, Angel, and MJ hands. Zea steps forward in a protective manner as they all proceed. Upon meeting Lady O, she agrees to grant the kids' wishes and requests. But before she does, she has one small favor. They must go to "The Lost World" and bring back the Magic Medallion which hangs around the neck, of Elvia Queen of Soul. If that's what it takes for Zea to get back to Bay Village, for Gia to find her heart, MJ's courage, Angel's, intellect, and Choir Boy's profound faith, then let the games begin. Reluctantly they all concur. In preparation for their journey, an image of the Mysterious Stranger appears in Zea's magical watch with safety instructions. "Push this button here only in an extreme emergency." "When in danger, press this red button.", points Galena. Zea nods with confirmations. "These devices will allow all of you to swim the oceans and walk the land.", explains General Galena.

LOST WORLD LOST GIRLS

Entering the Lost World, the kids didn't notice that the 'Welcome to The Lost World' sign had mysteriously changed to 'DANGER' as they pass by. They are greeted by four incredibly attractive young girls singing in a nearby lagoon. "Hello, we are the Lost Girls.", all speaking in unison. The boys may have been mesmerized by The Lost Girls song, but Gia and Baby Girl are not buying it and are still very suspicious.

In a flash, The Lost Girls transform into beautiful mermaids right before their very eyes. Before the boys could react, The Lost Girls are grabbing them off the shoreline and dragging them into the depths of the deep ocean. Gia sees what is going on and runs towards the beach but is tackled by one of The Lost Girls posted up onshore watching her. Gia and Baby Girl are dragged down into the dark sea as well.

ZERZOO &
LAND OF BOO
"an urban fairy tale"

CHAPTER III

"WHY DO PEOPLE HAVE TO DIE?"

King Nino and Queen Elvia watch from the castle deep in the underwater world. Queen Elvia has ordered The Lost Girls to capture the group and "Bring them to me!", she commands. After bringing the kids to the castle, the King and Queen inform them that no one can help them now. Both monarchs point to a large number 24 projected on the wall, confirming to kids that they have only 24 hours to live. Zea, Gia and Baby Girl are placed in separate cells. Choir Boy, Angel, and MJ are all placed in another. MJ, being a master at picking locks, quickly unlocks the door freeing the trio. They search through the castle looking for their other friends. Choir Boy who has taken a different path stumbles upon Gia and Baby Girl's cell. Angel and MJ locate Zea and free him too. The guards realizing, they have escaped sound the alarm and the hunt is on. Terrified, the kids start to run but they are completely surrounded. The King and Queen of Soul appear perched high on a cliff. Queen Elvia pointing her finger at Zea shoot a lightning bolt from her fingertips striking him once. Choir Boy anticipating extreme danger jumps in front of Zea taking on the second more powerful deadly ray. It hits him in his chest. Crying out in pain, he grabs his heart and disappears. "OH MY GOD! YOU KILLED CHOIR BOY!", screams Gia and Baby Girl. "HE'S DEAD!", shouts Angel.

VENGEANCE IS MINE OR MAYBE NOT

Zea is overwhelmed by what he has just witnessed and is upset. Looking down in disbelief, his best friend, his homeboy is gone - dead... It's his entire fault. Remembering what the Mysterious Stranger told him, Zea presses the "red button" on his magical watch. As he pushes the button which holds all the powers of the universe, a brilliant burst of lights and colors appear. It's Magnolia a little shaken but alive! She was thought to have been dead up until now. Her abrupt appearance surprises everyone. Yelling for everyone to "STOP!", she explains that everything was a big misunderstanding. Zea was a victim of the Karina Hurricane disaster and lost his family and friends too. The destruction was a part of global warming. It was a natural disaster that actually killed Queen Crystal - King Nino's wife. Sadden and hurt by what they had just heard, King Nino and Queen Elvia started to weep. Boo Security, the SeaWeeds begin to uncontrollably cry too. Everyone begins to cry and hug and say I'm sorry to each other.

Miraculously at that moment, Queen Crystal too mysteriously appears to their delight. She had not been killed after all. Between all the uncontrollable rejoicing, it was concluded that the right thing to do, was to formally present Zea and the kids with Queen Elvia's Magic Black Medallion. It is her way of gifting to them her appreciation and everlasting friendship. It was decided they would all go back to the Capitol City to celebrate and attend Zea's going home party.

The Mysterious Stranger's image appears. He tells them the secret of the Magic Black Medallion. "Honor and respect your family and friends - especially your mother and father. Never take love and kindness for weakness. All that glitters is not bling-bling. And money can't buy you love." Now knowing the secret of the Magic Black Medallion, returning home to Bay Village is bittersweet. Zea had befriended the King and Queen of Soul, and retrieved the Magic Black Medallion for Enchantress O. How much more could they be forced to endure? They were just kids for heaven's sake. Zea is again speechless without words and confused. Thinking to himself, "Why do people die? Why did Choir Boy have to die?" Choir Boy was his moral compass and truly his very best friend. He pauses to ponder and then pray. After a few moments, before he takes one step he mumbles, "Why do people have to die? To make life important...

ATLANTIS EAST

The celebration in the Land of Boo is in full swing with all the grandeur and pageantry of a royal affair is everywhere. The crew has been granted their wishes. Gia gets a "Gold Heart" representing her heart of gold, MJ a "Purple Heart" for courage and bravery, and Angel an MBA degree from Boo University, for his high intellect.

Enchantress O invites Zea to stay and reign as King in Boo forever but he must get back to Bay Village. Zea explains he had learned, while in the Land of Boo that "money can't buy you love." He witnessed that the "grass is not always greener on the other side" and "all that glitters is not gold". That the love and respect of your family and friends are the most important things of all. Because of his newfound wisdom, he would respectfully decline this huge honor bestowed upon him. Anticipating his answer, Enchantress O has one more gift for the brave boy. At that moment, Beyonce Airlines comes into full view and lands. Lady O has decided that she and General Galena, along with Boo Security and the Royal Court will personally take Zea back to the land above the sea. She has invited Gia, Baby Girl, Angel, and MJ to accompany them for an all-expense paid round trip adventure. Everyone is overjoyed and ecstatic about the invitation and journey.

Undetected during all the excitement, EyesWorth Green, Willie Popcorn along with Boo Security Forces, do not see X and his gang sneak onto Beyonce Air and board early. Zea, all of his new friends, the King and Queen of Soul, along with Queen Crystal, Magnolia, and others board the aircraft with anticipation and prepare for takeoff. The plane taxies down the runway and lifts. The ascend was flawless.

The cheering crowd can be heard in a distance. The residents of Boo all waving good-by enthusiastically.

As Beyonce Airline's vessel starts to penetrate the natural barrier of the two dimensions that divide the lands above and below the sea, something goes wrong! Fire erupts across the sky. In a flash, there is a mid-air explosion, and the aircraft blows up! Hysterical screams can be heard from the amazed Boo land citizens. Pointing towards what once was Beyonce Air, one resident can be heard saying, among the cries and moans, "Why do people have to die?" All are now watching in horror, as if in slow-motion, the fireball explosion, and total disintegration of the Beyonce Airlines' aircraft. Screams and loud cries of agony are forever frozen in time. Within the chaos, you hear the sound of a heartbeat, strong and loud at first, then becoming fainter and fainter and slower as time goes on. Then the heartbeat stops, the sound of flat lining fills the air. And then nothing - just silence...

BACK IN BAY VILLIAGE

Back in Bay Village at the Blue home once again a voice screams, "Why do people have to die?" It's Ms. Blue having a nervous breakdown, being assisted by Mr. Blue and the other neighbors. Miraculously lying in a large room that has been turned into a hospital and recovery center is a row of beds. In those beds are coma recovery victims of the hurricane. For the first time in a year, upon hearing his mother's distraught voice, Zea slowly opens his eyes and focuses on his distraught parents, followed by Mika, Essay, Magic, Paula, Kennedy, and Choir Boy. Choir Boy who after opening his eyes last, simply pats his heart and points to the heavens. All replied to Mrs. Blue in unison, "To make life important!!!" Also, in beds recovering, surprisingly are Bennie Boo, his B-Boys, and Rasta Man, who were all presumed dead but had all been in a coma up until this very moment. They all Rejoiced. Perplexed Zea and his friends look at each other with spooky expressions. Zea starts to hum the "Twilight Zone" theme song. Everyone laughs they embrace each other and all cry tears of joy.

THERE'S NO PLACE LIKE HOME

It's Saturday evening and all are having dinner at the family restaurant Magnolia Sea Food. In walks Rasta Man and motions for Zea to meet him in another room - away and out of sight of the others. Rasta Man places a lost mysterious package in Zea's hands. Rasta Man winks as he begins to walk out the back door. Zea invites him to come in to meet and join his family. Reluctantly, Rasta Man agrees, taking his place at the table and everyone welcomes him. During that time Zea secretly passes the mysterious package to Bennie Boo. Bennie Boo privately unwraps the package first with no expression then casts a sly smile. In the small box is a beautiful Black Safire Medallion. After a deep breath and sigh Bennie Boo quickly wraps it back up and puts it in his pocket. He nods in approval with a childish grin. His gold tooth sparkles in the light.

What the kids did not know, is that Bennie Boo had mistakenly robbed a house in the French Quarters and stolen the Black Safire Medallion weeks ago. To his amazement, the house belonged to Crystal, Bay Village's High Princess. She had placed a spell on him and would not take it off until he returned her sacred medallion, which had been passed down in her family for generations. She had threatened to change Bennie Boo into a "donkey" in 24 hours - if he did not return her property. Afraid to return it himself, because he had heard that his homeboy Willie Popcorn had crossed Crystal, and no one has seen or heard from him ever since. They say she has magical powers, and he would have never taken it if he knew it belonged to Crystal. Bennie had gotten Zea, an unassuming guy to do his dirty work, knowing that Crystal would not hurt an innocent kid. What they did not know, is that Crystal was not a voodoo princess, but an actual American Indian princess and the Black Safire Medallion had no real magic powers at all. It was an ancient family air loom that was precious and very sentimental to her.

Rasta Man enters and motions to Zea. He tells Zea that he has returned the Black Safire Medallion to Crystal. Bennie Boo and Zea are off the hook. Bennie Boo and the B-Boys, Pookie, and Ray-Ray enter and offer Zea their apologies and friendship denouncing the gang life altogether. Rasta Man continues to explain that Lady Crystal is not a voodoo princess but an authentic American Indian Princess and heir to a grand ancient dynasty. The medallion was passed down from generation to generation and is a priceless American artifact. Next door at Magnolia Sea Food restaurant the families are arriving to celebrate. It's Mardi Gras and the famous traditional parades and festivities are about to kick-off!

The sound of Jazz music fills the air. It could only mean one thing to the residents of Bay Village. *"Let The Good Times Roll!"*

Grand and lavish "Friends of the Sea" themed beautifully decorated floats approach Zea and the crew. Putting on his glasses to get a better view, Zea is stunned and bewildered at what he sees riding down Bourbon Street, in BAY VILLAGE!

Encased in a virtual Land of Boo themed float, sitting on golden thrones are Nino and Elvia The King and Queen of Soul! In tow are Queen Crystal, the Boo Royal Security Force, EyesWorth Green, and Willie Popcorn, along with the SeaWeeds waving, winking, and throwing Mardi gras beads to the stunned children, of Bay Village. It is followed by a second Mardi Gras underwater paradise themed float. Riding with pride is King Fish, his golden grill (smile) glowing in the sun. Bubbles the Whale, the official Boo Press Secretary, and The Lost Girls all blowing kisses and throwing magic beads to ZeaZoo and all the children of Bay Village. On the back of the last Mardi Gras float, as it travels into the distance, Zea cleans his glasses to make sure he is correctly reading what he thought he was reading. In big bold letters, sparkling in the warm Gulf Coast sun it read, Land of Boo, Lost Girls, No Secrets...

THE END?

Join the *LAND OF BOO FAN CLUB*

by Subscribing to our VIP Newsletter Today!

Win Cool Gifts, Gear and Prizes

EMAIL: FamilyFilm1@aol.com